P9-DMW-337

Ollie's Easter Eggs

Written and illustrated by
Olivier Dunrea

Houghton Mifflin Books for Children
HOUGHTON MIFFLIN HARCOURT
Boston New York 2009

Copyright © 2009 by Olivier Dunrea

All rights reserved. For information about permission to reproduce selections from this book, write to Permissions, Houghton Mifflin Harcourt Publishing Company, 215 Park Avenue South, New York, New York 10003.

Houghton Mifflin Books for Children is an imprint of
Houghton Mifflin Harcourt Publishing Company.

www.hmhbooks.com

The text of this book is set in 24-point Shannon.
The illustrations are ink and watercolor on paper.

Library of Congress Cataloging-in-Publication Data
Dunrea, Olivier.
Ollie's easter eggs / by Olivier Dunrea.
p. cm.
Summary: Ollie watches the other goslings dye and hide eggs for the Easter hunt, but no one can find the eggs when Ollie decides that they are all for him.
ISBN 0-618-53243-9 (hardcover)
[1. Geese—Fiction. 2. Easter eggs—Fiction. 3. Easter—Fiction.] I. Title.
PZ7.D922Op 2006
[E]—dc22
2004026552

Printed in Singapore

TWP 10 9 8 7 6 5 4 3 2 1

To Anita and Lin–
who shared many Easter
egg hunts with m

This is Gossie and Gertie.
They are gathering eggs.

This is BooBoo and Peedie.
They are gathering eggs, too.

This is Ollie.

He is hopping.

Gossie dyes her egg
bright red.

Gertie dyes her egg
bright blue.

BooBoo dyes her egg
bright purple.

Peedie dyes his egg
bright yellow.

Ollie stares at the
brightly colored eggs.

"I want eggs!" he shouts.

Gossie hides her egg
in the green grass.

"My egg," whispers Ollie.
He rolls the red egg out of sight.

Gertie hides her egg
in the yellow straw.

"My egg," whispers Ollie.
He rolls the blue egg out of sight.

BooBoo hides her egg
in the red tulips.

"My egg," whispers Ollie.
He rolls the purple egg out of sight.

Peedie hides his egg
under the green turtle.

"My egg," whispers Ollie.
He rolls the yellow egg out of sight.

Ollie hides all the eggs
under his blanket.

Gossie and Gertie hunt
for the Easter eggs.
They look in the tulips.

They look under the turtle.

BooBoo and Peedie hunt
for the Easter eggs.
They look in the grass.

They look in the straw.

Gossie and Gertie
scoot past Ollie.

Searching. Hunting.

BooBoo and Peedie
scurry past Ollie.

Hunting. Searching.

"Look!" Ollie says.
Four small goslings stop and stare.
"Easter eggs!" shouts Ollie.